# Phoebe Gilman

# A Treasury of
# Jillian Jiggs

Scholastic Canada Ltd.
Toronto  New York  London  Auckland  Sydney
Mexico City  New Delhi  Hong Kong  Buenos Aires

**Scholastic Canada Ltd.**
604 King Street West, Toronto, Ontario M5V 1E1, Canada

**Scholastic Inc.**
557 Broadway, New York, NY 10012, USA

**Scholastic Australia Pty Limited**
PO Box 579, Gosford, NSW 2250, Australia

**Scholastic New Zealand Limited**
Private Bag 94407, Greenmount, Auckland, New Zealand

**Scholastic Children's Books**
Euston House, 24 Eversholt Street, London NW1 1DB, UK

**Library and Archives Canada Cataloguing in Publication**
Gilman, Phoebe, 1940-2002.
A treasury of Jillian Jiggs / written and illustrated by Phoebe Gilman.

Contents: Jillian Jiggs -- The wonderful pigs of Jillian Jiggs --
Jillian Jiggs to the rescue -- Jillian Jiggs and the secret surprise --
Jillian Jiggs and the great big snow.
ISBN-13 978-0-545-99316-6

I. Title.

PS8563.I54T74 2008          jC813'.54          C2007-907187-2

ISBN-10 0-545-99316-4

6 5 4 3 2 1          Printed in Singapore          08 09 10 11 12 13

# Contents

# Jillian Jiggs

A long time ago, when she was quite small,
Jilian Jiggs wore nothing at all.

"Those were the days," her mother would sigh,
As she looked round the room and started to cry.
For Jillian Jiggs liked to dress up and play,
And this made a mess in her room every day.

"Jillian, Jillian, Jillian Jiggs!
It looks like your room has been lived in by pigs!"

"Later. I promise. As soon as I'm through,
I'll clean up my room. I promise. I do."

Now, Jillian meant every word that she said,
But later the promise flew out of her head.
When Rachel and Peter started to shout,
Jillian had to, just had to go out.

"Oh, look at the boxes! Yippee! Hooray!
It's hard to believe someone threw these away.
I'm mad about boxes. Boxes are fun.
No one will guess who we are when we're done."

No one would guess . . .

But a mother would know.
A mother could tell by the tip of a toe.

"Jillian, Jillian, Jillian Jiggs!
It looks like your room has been lived in by pigs!"

"Later. I promise. As soon as I'm through,
I'll clean up my room. I promise. I do."

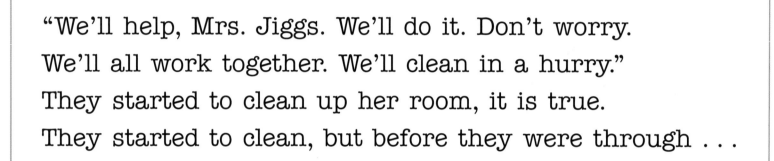

"We'll help, Mrs. Jiggs. We'll do it. Don't worry.
We'll all work together. We'll clean in a hurry."
They started to clean up her room, it is true.
They started to clean, but before they were through . . .

Jillian thought up a game that was new.
They had to stop cleaning. What else could they do?

"Let's dress up as pirates. Tie sails to the bed.
Heave ho, you landlubbers! Full speed ahead!"

They dressed up as dragons.

They dressed up as trees.

They dressed up as bad guys who never say please.

They dressed up as chickens, cooped up and caged.

They turned into monsters who hollered and raged.

They cackled like witches. They stirred and they boiled.

Then they were royalty, pampered and spoiled.

They tiptoed and twirled like little light fairies.

They made themselves wings and flew like canaries.

Whenever they thought that was it, they were through . . .

She'd change all their costumes and start something new.

Then Jillian's mother came in with her mop,

Took one look around and . . .

...fainted, KERPLOP!

"Jillian, Jillian, Jillian Jiggs!
It looks like your room has been lived in by pigs!"

"Later. I promise. As soon as I'm ... "

"Start cleaning this minute, this second, not later!
I want this room tidy. I want this room straighter!"

"You'd better go now, Rachel and Peter.
See you tomorrow when everything's neater."

# The Wonderful Pigs of Jillian Jiggs

A long time ago, as you may recall,
Jillian Jiggs never cleaned up at all.

"Jillian, Jillian, Jillian Jiggs!
It looks like your room has been lived in by pigs!"

Well, wonder of wonders, without any warning,
Jillian cleaned up one Saturday morning.
She made her room tidy and neat as a pin.

"Can this really be Jillian's room that I'm in?"

43

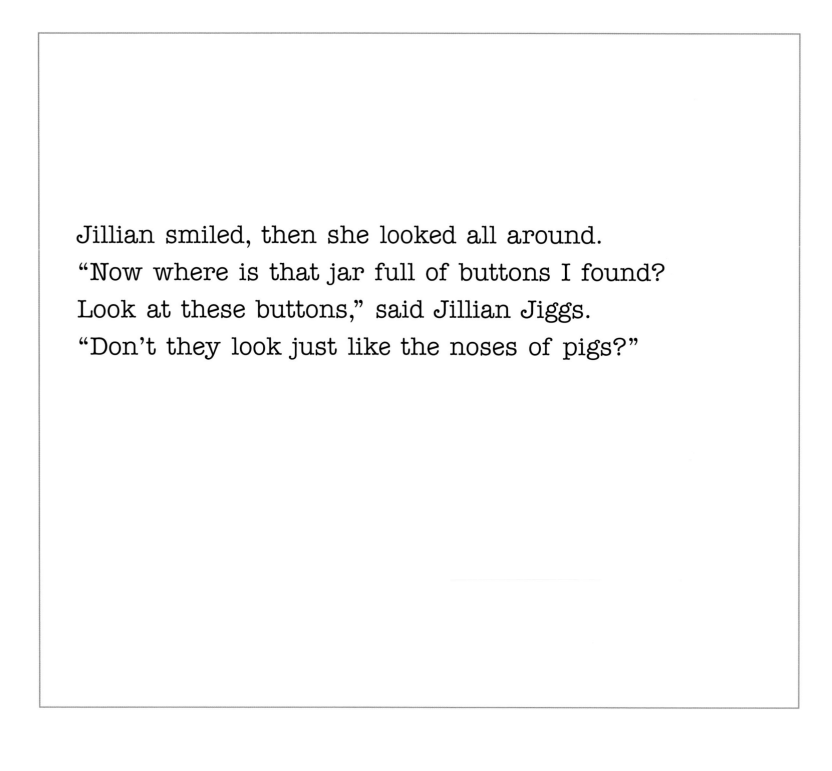

Jillian smiled, then she looked all around.
"Now where is that jar full of buttons I found?
Look at these buttons," said Jillian Jiggs.
"Don't they look just like the noses of pigs?"

"We'll make little pigs and then set up a store.
I'm sure we can sell at least fifty or more.
We'll make lots of money, we'll be billionaires!
Then Mother can rest and forget all her cares."

Once Jillian started, she zipped right along,
Turning out piggies while singing this song:

"Jillian, Jillian, Jillian Jiggs,
Maker of wonderful, marvelous pigs!"

The first little pig had a sweet, smiling face.
The second she dressed up in old-fashioned lace.
And then she decided to give them both names.
She called one Clarissa, the other one James.

The next little pig had a hat and a cane.
His name was George and his girlfriend was Jane.
Miranda had red cheeks and long, dark eyelashes.
McTavish was old and had drooping mustaches.

She made up a pirate pig, Blackberry Billy,
To play with her princess pig, Lavender Lilly.

"Jillian, Jillian, Jillian Jiggs!
Maker of wonderful, marvelous pigs!"

A striped pig named Dudley, a plaid pig named Sue.

A family of Martian pigs, Beep, Bop and Boo.

She might still be sitting there, sewing away,
Except Rachel and Peter came over to play.

"Hi, Rachel! Hi, Peter! Quick, come on in.
Guess what I'm making," she said with a grin.

They couldn't believe it — pigs, pigs galore,
Were scattered all over the bed, desk and floor.

"Jillian, Jillian, Jillian Jiggs,
Your room REALLY looks like it's lived in by pigs!"

They gathered them up and they took them all out.
They made up a sign and they marched all about.
"Jillian, Jillian, Jillian Jiggs,

Maker of wonderful, marvelous pigs!
Ten cents a pig, not one penny more.
They're waiting for you at Jillian's store."

They came to buy pigs. They came by the dozens.
Brothers and sisters, best friends and cousins.

Was Jillian happy?

Now here's a sad tale.

How could she put all her pigs up for sale?

"Oh, no, not Marlene! She's so cute and so cuddly.
And not my Clarissa or Rosie or Dudley.
I can't give up Marvin, he'd miss his friend Thomas.
I'll never sell him, I gave him my promise."

"No, no, not McTavish, I can't let HIM go.
And Blackberry Billy would miss me, you know.
I can't sell poor Gregory, he has the flu.
He should stay in bed for the next day or two."

"I simply can't do it. It's over. I'm through . . . "

Then all of a sudden she knew what to do.

"Step right up, friends! Have lots of fun!
Sew your own pigs! Learn how it's done!
We'll make hundreds and millions and zillions of pigs!"

said wonderful, marvelous Jillian Jiggs.

# Instructions
# for making a wonderful pig

## Materials

| | |
|---|---|
| Old stocking . . . . . . . . . . . . . . . . . . . . . . . . . . . . | any colour. Wonderful pigs come in all colours! |
| Needle and thread . . . . . . . . . . . . . . . . . . . . . | to sew your pig. |
| Polyester fibrefill . . . . . . . . . . . . . . . . . . . . . | for stuffing. You wouldn't want a skinny pig! |
| Embroidery floss . . . . . . . . . . . . . . . . . . . . . | to sew your pig's eyes and mouth. |
| Felt . . . . . . . . . . . . . . . . . . . . . . . . . . . . | to make ears so that your pig can hear you. |
| Yarn . . . . . . . . . . . . . . . . . . . . . . . . . . . . | unless you want a bald pig. |
| Button . . . . . . . . . . . . . . . . . . . . . . . . . . . | for your pig's nose. |
| Pipe cleaners . . . . . . . . . . . . . . . . . . . . . . | if your pig is a Martian pig. |
| Lace and ribbon . . . . . . . . . . . . . . . . . . . . | for a fancy pig. |
| Pink crayon . . . . . . . . . . . . . . . . . . . . . . . | for colouring rosy cheeks on your pig. |
| Scissors and glue | |

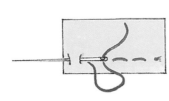
running stitch

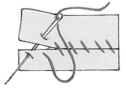
whip stitch

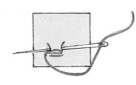
fastening thread

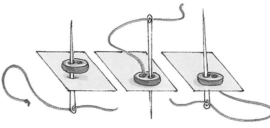
sewing on a button

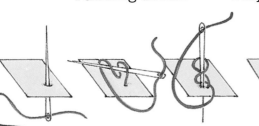
french knot

surprised mouth

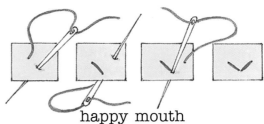
happy mouth

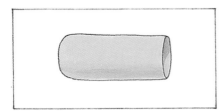
1. Cut one piece of stocking
25 cm (10") long.

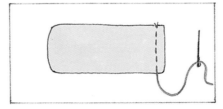
2. Sew a row of running
stitches around one end
of the stocking.

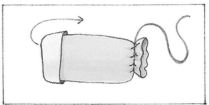
3. Pull thread tight to gather.
Fasten and cut thread, then
turn the stocking inside-out.

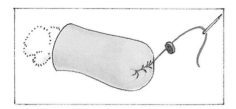

4. Stuff the head with fibrefill. Sew a button on in the middle of the stitching line.

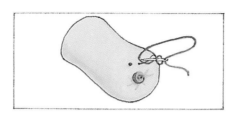

5. Bring the needle and embroidery floss up from the inside and sew french knots for the eyes.

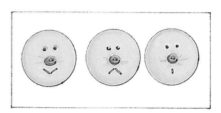

6. Sew a happy or mad or surprised mouth.

7. Cut two triangles of felt for the ears. Use the whip stitch to sew them in place.

8. Add more stuffing for the body, placing four balls of stuffing inside, underneath, for the feet.

9. Tie thread around the balls from outside to complete the feet.

10. Twist the remainder of the stocking to make a curly tail.

11. Tie the end in a knot.

Glue or sew on yarn or fibrefill for hair, mustaches or beards. Add ribbon and lace for fancy pigs. Poke in bits of pipe cleaner for Martian pigs. Colour your pig's cheeks rosy.

Give your pig a name and say, "Welcome to my family!"

# Jillian Jiggs
## to the Rescue

For Peggy and
Tom Bender

The moon had just risen high over the hill.
The stars were all out. It was quiet and still.
But instead of the sound of snoring and sleeping,
Jillian Jiggs heard somebody weeping.

"I'm scared of the monster," said her little sister. Jillian held her and Jillian kissed her.

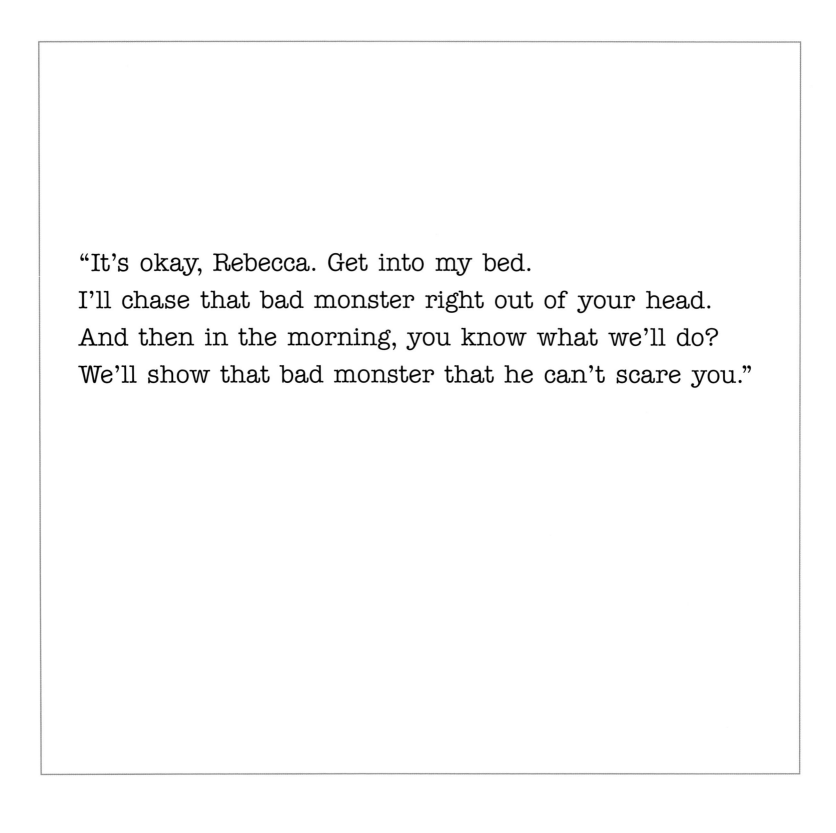

"It's okay, Rebecca. Get into my bed.
I'll chase that bad monster right out of your head.
And then in the morning, you know what we'll do?
We'll show that bad monster that he can't scare you."

And this is what happened the very next day,
When Rachel and Peter came over to play.

"Hi, Rachel! Hi, Peter! Quick, get inside.
The monster might catch you," Jillian cried.
"He's scaring Rebecca. He's mangy. He's MEAN!
To stop him we're making . . .

. . . a MONSTER MACHINE!

This monster machine will shrink him so small,

He'll be squished. He'll be squashed.

He'll be nothing at all."

"We'll help," Peter said. "Four is better than two.

You never can tell what a monster might do."

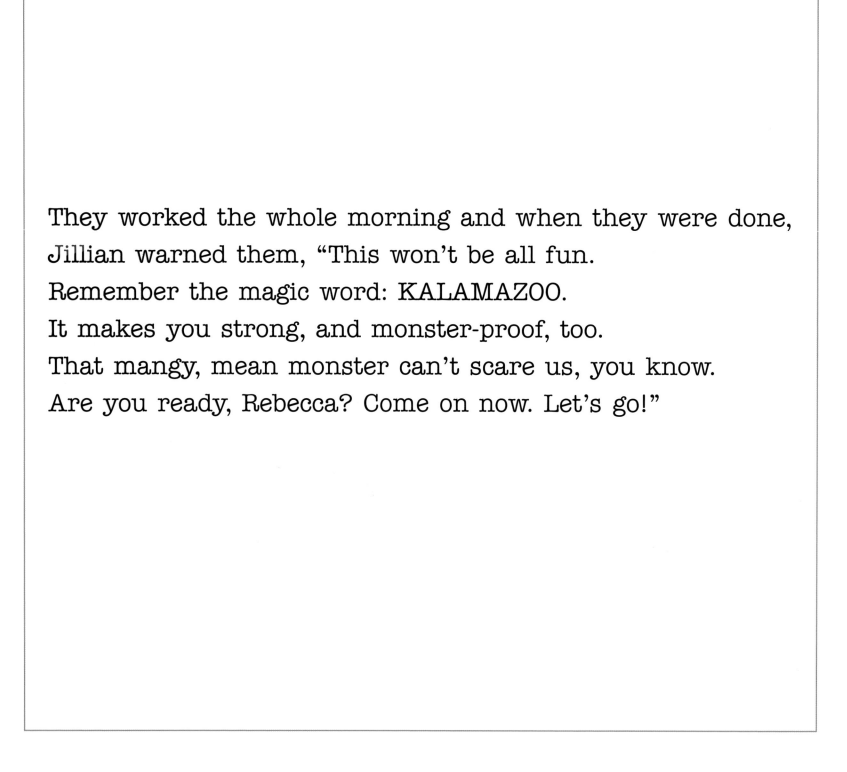

They worked the whole morning and when they were done,
Jillian warned them, "This won't be all fun.
Remember the magic word: KALAMAZOO.
It makes you strong, and monster-proof, too.
That mangy, mean monster can't scare us, you know.
Are you ready, Rebecca? Come on now. Let's go!"

"Kalamazoo! Kalamazoo!
Monster, you're meatloaf! Monster, you're through!

Our monster machine will shrink you so small,
You'll be squished. You'll be squashed.
You'll be nothing at all."

They had to be sneaky and circle around,
Looking for clues that lay deep underground.

They followed the tracks. They were fearless and steady.
They never gave up. They were rough, tough and ready.

"Kalamazoo! Kalamazoo!
Monster, you're meatloaf. Monster, you're through!

Our monster machine will shrink you so small,
You'll be squished. You'll be squashed.
You'll be nothing at all."

The monster was clever, he kept out of sight.
He knew he'd be stronger much later . . . at night!
But deep in the forest, the road turned and dipped,

And he wasn't careful. He stumbled and tripped.
"Shh!" said Rebecca. "Did you hear that thumping?
Look over there, the bushes are bumping."

"It's him. It's the monster. He's lurking in there,"
Said Jillian Jiggs. "Better BEWARE!"

"Oh, no!" said Rebecca. "Remember, he's mean!
This looks like a job for the monster machine!"

They filled a big pot with some green grass and dirt,
And smushed it together for monster dessert!

The pot was then left by the monster machine
And all of them hid where they couldn't be seen.

"Get down," said Rebecca. "The monster's awake."

The monster came nearer. They felt the ground shake.
Nearer and nearer until . . .

. . . the box SNAPPED!

"Aha!" said Rebecca. "Monster, you're trapped!"

"Kalamazoo! Kalamazoo!
Monster, you're meatloaf. Monster, you're through!
Our monster machine will shrink you so small,
You'll be squished. You'll be squashed.
You'll be nothing at all."

They switched the great switch on the monster machine. "We'll squish-squash him down to the size of a bean!" The clickers were clicking. The lights started blinking.

"Yes!" said Rebecca. "The monster is shrinking."

"Monster, O Monster, why are you mean?
Why do you roar and shout in her dream?
Monster, O Monster, why are you bad?"

"I think," said Rebecca, "I think that he's sad.
He might have been lonely, he needs friends like you.
He might have been angry and that's why he grew."

"We'd better shrink him a little bit more.
Then he won't scare you like he did before."

"Stop!" said Rebecca. "Enough is enough."

They didn't listen, they kept acting tough.
They didn't listen. They kept right on going,
The squishing and squashing showed no sign of slowing.
Then the monster machine began bumping about.

"Look," said Rebecca, "he wants to get out! Can't we be friends? Can't he play too?"

The monster agreed. The monster said . . .

"Mew."

# Jillian Jiggs
## and the
## Secret Surprise

For the new kids
on the block

Ariana    Emily    Matthew

Connor    Morgan    Griffin

Sammy    Jacob    Rachel

Derian

The streamers flip-flapped in the soft summer breeze.

Balloons bobbed and bounced on the branches of trees.

But Jillian sat on the steps feeling sad.

"Oh, I'm a bad sister. Oh, I'm bad bad bad.

I can't buy a present. I haven't a cent.

How did it happen? My money's all spent."

"Jillian Jiggs," Rachel said to her friend,
"Stop moaning and groaning. This isn't the end.
Take my advice, and make no mistake:
The best birthday present is one that you make."

"She's right," Peter said. "And I'm counting on you
To think up a present for me to give, too."

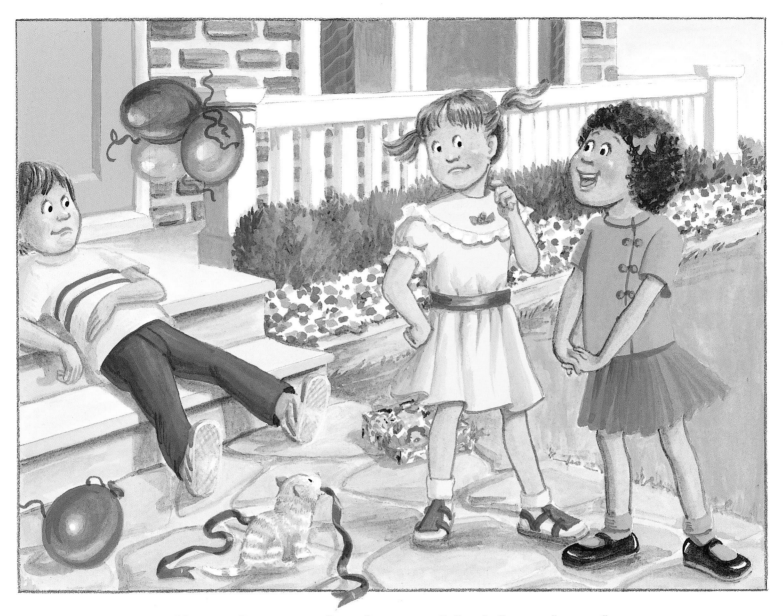

As Jillian listened, she nodded her head.
"You think I can do it? I'll do it!" she said.
"How about this? We could put on a show.
We'll plan it in secret. Rebecca won't know
What we are doing until it's all done."

"I like that," said Rachel. "Surprises are fun."

A few dabs of paint and a doodad or two
Made old clothes and boxes look magically new.
At last they were ready. Rehearsals began.
But things didn't happen according to plan.

For while they were busy rehearsing the show,
Nobody bothered to look out below.

They didn't see that Rebecca's friend Shirley
Had come to the party a little too early.

"I want to be in the birthday show, too.
I want to be a great actor like you."

"Oh, no!" Rachel said. "That's the end of our fun.
The surprise will be over before it's begun."

They looked at Shirley, then looked at each other.
And Shirley became the new Royal Queen Mother.

"Okay, now that's settled," Jillian said.
She hadn't noticed that Molly and Fred
Had watched Shirley put on her jewels and her crown.

"That isn't fair," Molly said and sat down.
"We want to be in the birthday show, too.
We want to be famous actors like you."

So Peter invented a dragon named Quizzle,
With scaly green spikes and a frightening sizzle.
But neither one would be the dragon's rear end.

"You would change places if you were my friend."

Jillian said, "There is no need to fight.
The beast has two heads. There is no end in sight."

They snorted and roared and breathed fiery breath.
They sizzled and fried and scared Peter to death.

"Okay. Now that's settled," Jillian said.
"On with the show!" and she nodded her head.

But nothing was settled. In fact, things got messy.
When she turned around — there was Sarah and Jesse.

"We want to be in the birthday show, too.
We want to be famous actors like you."

The cast just kept growing. It didn't take long
Before things began to go even more wrong.

"We want a part," Mark and Emily cried.
"It isn't fun to be shuffled aside."

"Please. Pretty please," Max and Natalie pleaded.
"There must be a small part where we would be needed."

Jillian told them they had to be quiet.
But they wouldn't listen. They started to riot.

"We want to be in the birthday show, too.
We want to be famous actors like you."

The guests wouldn't go to the party. They'd whine,
Or climb on the stage and say, "This side is fine."

Jillian said, "What a tough situation.
I'll need more parts than my first calculation."

Peter just shrugged and said, "Jillian Jiggs,
All this play needs is a chorus of pigs!"

"Yes!" the guests shouted. "Oink, oink, hooray!"

Jillian nodded. "Then on with the play!
Now we are ready. No more can be done."
That's when she heard the words . . .

"Where's everyone?"

"Oh, no! It's Rebecca. What'll I do?
She shouldn't see this until we are through."

"Jillian, Jillian, let me play, too."

"This isn't a game. It's my present for you."

"You say it's my present? Then hold on a minute.
Today is MY birthday. I want to be in it."

And that's how Rebecca became the star mouse
Who led the whole cast to the back of the house.

There they fixed up a stage and got set to begin.
The curtains were opened. The chorus came in.
And then they stopped . . .

. . . because no one was there.
All that they saw was just chair after chair.

"What'll we do? What kind of a show
Has no one to watch it? We'd like to know!"

Jillian gulped and said, "Quick, close the curtain.
I've thought of someone, and I'm very certain
That SHE will not want to be part of the show.
She will be happy to sit down. I know.
Okay, everybody. Now, please, close your eyes.
I'm going to get the last birthday . . . "

# "SURPRISE!"

(This is the end, but if you want more,
Put on your own play. Bravo! Encore!
Want to know how? It's easy. Just look
At Jillian's play: it comes next in this book.)

# Jillian Jiggs

## Presents

# The Chicken Princess

# *The Cast*
## in order of appearance:

**Queen**

**Hero**

**Chorus**
*(as many people as you like)*

**Dave the Giant**

**Mouse**

**Dragon**
*(with as many heads as you like)*

**Wizard**

**Princess**

If you have more actors they can appear, in a variety of costumes,
in the magic wand scene in Act III.

For costume, prop and staging tips check out Phoebe Gilman's website: www.phoebegilman.com

# ACT I
## The Queen's Castle

**CHORUS**
A wild wind is blowing, OO WOO all around.
The trees are all frosted. Snow covers the ground.
The curtain is opened. Now let us begin.
Here is the castle. Queen Esther comes in.

*The curtain opens on the inside of a castle room.
There is a mop propped against the wall.*

**QUEEN**
Alas! Woe is me! That evil, mean Wizard
Has stolen the Princess away in the blizzard.

*The Hero enters.*

**HERO**
Forsooth! Never fear! And do not be sad.
I am the Hero and I'm really mad.
I am the Hero and I'll save the day.
That is the reason that I'm in this play.

**QUEEN**
Without my sweet child, life has no meaning.
Now I must go. The castle needs cleaning.

*She reaches for the mop.*

**QUEEN**
Oh, by the way, you know about Dave,
The rather large giant who watches the cave?

*The Hero shakes his head, looking worried.*

**QUEEN**
You don't? Now you do. Better take care.
Look out for Dave, when you get there.

*The Queen exits. The Hero speaks before
exiting too.*

**HERO**
Farewell! I am going out in the blizzard.
I'll rescue the Princess and capture the Wizard.

*The curtain closes. When it re-opens, we see a snowy
landscape with a cave. The Hero runs in place.*

**CHORUS**
*(makes wind sounds: Ooo woo! Ooo woo! etc.)*

**HERO**
Brr. I am freezing. This cold wind doth blast.
I'm trying to run, but it's hard to move fast.

**CHORUS**
*(to the audience)*
Our Hero needs help. Can you stomp your feet,
As if you were running? But stay in your seat.

*The Hero runs faster in place.*

**HERO**
What's that I see there? A dark, gloomy cave.
I don't see the Wizard, and I don't see Dave.

**GIANT**
*(aside to the audience)*
Of course he won't see me, until it's too late,
Because I am hiding. Isn't that great?

**HERO**
*(lifts up two paper footprints)*
I smell a rat and it doesn't smell sweet.
Footprints are here, but there are no feet.
I've nerves of steel and I shall be brave.
I'm not afraid, but — where is this Dave?

*The Giant steps out with a foam rubber bat and bops
the Hero on the head, then drags him into the cave.*

# ACT II
## The Giant's Cave

*The cave is dimly lit. The Hero is inside a large cauldron.*

**GIANT**

Fee! I say, fie! And a fo fum and phooey!
Looks like I've caught something
  yummy and chewy.
He may be live, but soon he'll be dead.
Then I'll grind up his bones and make
  dead Hero bread!

**HERO**

How can this be? I've been popped in a pot.
If I am cooked, I won't like that a lot.

**CHORUS**

Our Hero is worried. He's very upset.
He shivers. He quivers. He breaks out in sweat.
Audience! Audience! Audience, please,
He needs some help. Say the magic word:
CHEESE!

*When the audience shouts "Cheese!" the Mouse tiptoes out on the stage.*

**MOUSE**

Squeak. Did you call me? O giant named Dave,
This isn't a nice way for you to behave.

**GIANT**

Eek! It's a mouse. O most foul brute!

**MOUSE**

Isn't that odd? I thought I was cute.

*The Giant backs away, frightened. The Mouse chases him offstage.*

**HERO**

  *(climbing out of the cauldron)*
Isn't it lucky that I was befriended?
Egads and gadzooks! The play might have ended.
There's no time to waste. I must find the Wizard.

**MOUSE**

Goodbye and good luck and —
Watch out for the lizard!

*The Mouse skips offstage as the lights dim. As the Hero speaks, the Dragon sneaks up behind him.*

**HERO**

I shall be brave — but it's black as the night.
I'm not afraid, but I wish it was light.

**DRAGON**

What's that you said? Did I hear the word light?
My fiery breath is both lovely and bright.

*The Dragon chases the Hero down through the audience, then corners him back onstage.*

**HERO**

Egads! How disgraceful to go to my death,
Sizzled and fried in a lizard's bad breath.

**CHORUS**

Our Hero is worried. He's starting to fry.
He sizzles. He frizzles. Alas! He may die.
Audience! Audience! Audience, please.
He needs some help. Say the magic word :

**AUDIENCE**
CHEESE!

*The Mouse tiptoes out, carrying a water squirter.*

**MOUSE**

Squeak. Did you call me, O volcanic lizard?
A squirt of cold water should cool that hot gizzard.

*The Mouse squirts water into
the Dragon's mouth (or mouths).*

**CHORUS**

*(makes sizzling sounds)*

**DRAGON**

My head! My poor head! I've a cold in my head.
My fire is out, so I guess I am dead.

*Dragon stumbles around, then crumples to the
floor.*

**MOUSE**

The Wizard awaits, and the maid in distress.
Watch out for the trap or you'll be in a mess.

*Storm effects: flashing lights, drums and cymbals.*

**HERO**

What's that I hear? Is that thunder and lightning?
I'm very brave . . . but . . . it is a bit frightening.

*The Wizard appears in a flash of lightning.*

**WIZARD**

There's no need to fear. I'm misunderstood!
See how I smile? I'm friendly. I'm good.

**HERO**

The Mouse was mistaken. He's not a bad chap.

*The Hero steps forward to shake his hand and is
caught in an invisible net.*

**HERO**

Oh no! I have tripped in a terrible trap!
The Wizard has cast an invisible net.
This isn't funny. I'm very upset.

*The lights go out. The curtain closes.*

# ACT III
## The Wizard's House

*Inside the Wizard's house. The Princess is in chains. The Hero is sitting in a squished position, still caught in the invisible net. A large, mysterious-looking book is sitting on a table, along with a key. Somewhere else on stage is a magic wand.*

**WIZARD**

Ha ha! You're all mine! Ah, Princess, you'll be
Someone to love and to take care of me.

**PRINCESS**

That's what you think, but it's very untrue.
I couldn't love someone as rotten as you.

**WIZARD**

   *(exiting)*

I'll get the ring and we'll set the date.
Your Hero can't save you. Yes, I am your fate!

**CHORUS**

Our Hero is crying. He's down on his knees.
He's shaking. He's quaking. He's starting
   to wheeze.
Audience! Audience! Audience, please.
He needs your help. Say the magic word:

**AUDIENCE**

CHEESE!

**MOUSE**

   *(appears, looking shocked)*

Squeak. Did you call me? Good gracious! I fear,
This could be the end of your Hero career!
With my sharp teeth, I shall bite through the net.
Don't cry, poor Hero. It's not over yet.

*The Mouse gnaws through the net and frees the Hero.*

**PRINCESS**

I'm still in these chains. Don't forget about me.
There isn't much time. Hand me that key!

*The Hero gets the key and unlocks the chain. The Princess, freed, opens the Wizard's large book and begins thumbing through it.*

**PRINCESS**

Now, go find his wand while I look for a spell.
Hmm. This one is nasty. Yes, this will do well.

*She mumbles to herself, memorizing. Meanwhile, the Hero searches on stage and down in the audience for the wand. Although the audience sees it clearly, he keeps missing it. The audience may shout encouragement and directions until he finds it.*

**HERO**

Aha! Here it is! Oh, I could grow fond,
Of swooshing around this wizardy wand.

*He waves the wand around. Lights flash as things, and any number of new characters, appear out of nowhere. Various sound effects are heard. Suddenly the lights go off and all is quiet.*

**CHORUS**

Egads and gadzooks!
How the play's plot doth thicken.
He's bewitched the Princess and now —

*The lights go on again. The Princess is in a chicken costume, the crown still on her head.*

**CHORUS**

She's a chicken!

Audience! Audience! Audience, please.
She needs your help. Say the magic word:

**AUDIENCE**
CHEESE!

**MOUSE**
Squeak! Did you call me? What's happened? Oh dear.
Give me that wand. She needs fixing. That's clear.

*The Mouse waves the wand. The lights go off. When they go on again, the Princess is her old self again.*

**PRINCESS**
Thank you. I thought I had run out of luck.
Imagine, a princess whose one word is "cluck"!
At last I am free. And before things get worse,
I'll take the wand and do my own verse.

*Takes the wand from the mouse.*

**PRINCESS**
Ssh! I hear footsteps. Get back in the net.

*The Princess winds the chain around her foot.
The Hero reluctantly gets back in the invisible net.*

**WIZARD**
  (offstage)
Princess. Oh, Princess. Where are you, my pet?

**PRINCESS**
Right where you left me. Come here, Wizard dear.
I have a secret I'd like you to hear.

*The Wizard enters with a large diamond ring. He closes his eyes and cups his ear to listen. The Princess leans toward him, the wand behind her back.*

**PRINCESS**
Oodle noodle. Kit kaboodle.
Sweetie pie, my own.

*She brings the wand forward and taps him on the head.*

**PRINCESS**
Toodle-oodle, apple strudel,
Now you're turned to stone.

*The Wizard freezes in his position. The other characters on stage dance joyously around him. The curtain closes.*

**CHORUS**
This is the end. There will be no more hassle.
They'll bring the statue back to the castle.

*The Hero steps out in front of the curtain and bows.*

**HERO**
The Princess is safe. The Queen is delighted.
And for my trouble, I shall be knighted.

*The Princess steps out in front of the curtain and curtsies.*

**PRINCESS**
Come on, everybody, back to my house.
It's time for my wedding. I'll marry —

*The Hero smiles and swaggers, as the Princess reaches through the closed curtains and brings forth the Mouse.*

**PRINCESS**
. . . The Mouse!!!

*The Mouse bows and reaches through the curtains, bringing forth the rest of the cast single file. When they are all assembled they bow in unison.*

The End

# Jillian Jiggs
## and the
# Great Big Snow

For two very special people,
Diane Kerner & Yüksel Hassan
XOXO

Silently, silently, all through the night,
Snowflakes had fallen, lacy and white.
By morning the town shimmered brilliant and new,
Promising wonderful, wild things to do.

Jillian Jiggs grabbed her toastiest clothes,
Pulled her woolliest socks up and over her toes,
Put on her sweater, her snow pants, and then,
Looked for her hat. It was missing again.

"Jillian, Jillian, say it's not true.
How do you lose all the things that you do?
You'd lose your head if it wasn't attached.
And where would I find you another that matched?"

"My hat isn't lost. It just hasn't been found.
Look — my scarf's long. I can wrap it around."

"No," said her mother. "Now go find your hat.
The weather's too cold to go outside like that."

Jillian searched every room, everywhere.
It had vanished, gone poof, disappeared in thin air.
She needed a hat and she needed it fast.
There was no time to waste, 'cause the snow might not last.

She opened her toy chest and pulled out some things:
A dragon, a mask and two butterfly wings.
Some boxes, a wand and a Martian hat too . . .

"I can't find THAT hat, but another might do."

"What do you think, Mom? Is this hat okay?
Mom . . . did you hear me? Can I go and play?"

Her mother stood up, took a deep breath and said,
"As long as it's warm and it stays on your head."

"Are you ready, Rebecca? Come on now, let's go!
Hop on the sled and we'll play in the snow."

Her friends took one look at the hat on her head:
"It's different," said Rachel. "It's weird," Peter said.

"My old hat is missing. I looked everywhere.
It vanished, went poof, disappeared in thin air.

When I couldn't find it, I took this instead.
So now I'm a Martian kid," Jillian said.

"Which means we're on Mars. And the Martians . . . Oh, no!
The Martians are stuck underneath all this snow!"

"We'll save them," said Peter. "We're smart and we're tough.
Come on. Let's get going. Start digging this stuff."

Little by little, they shovelled it clear,
And an alien landscape began to appear.
It had long, snaking roads and odd-looking hills,
And monsters to give you the shivers and chills.

One kind of creature had eyes on his snout,
And all that you saw was that snout sticking out
Of the door to his house, which was really a cave.
No one explored there unless they were brave.

Peter made one that had spikes on its tail.
Rachel's resembled a two-headed snail.

"My Martian's name is Thing-a-ma-bob.
He's small," said Rebecca, "and shaped like a blob."

"When these are finished they'll be Martian pigs.
I like pigs. They're friendly," said Jillian Jiggs.

"Jillian, Jillian, look, look! It's gone!
Where is the warm, woolly scarf you had on?"

They searched every hill, every cave, everywhere.

It had vanished, gone poof, disappeared in thin air.

"I'm in big trouble. When our mom finds out,
She'll fall down and faint, then she'll wake up and shout:

Jillian, Jillian, say it's not true!
How do you lose all the things that you do?"

"Are you going to stand around moping all day?
Come on now," said Rachel. "We're here to play!"

"You're right. Gone is gone," said Jillian Jiggs.
"I'm here on Mars and I'm making snow pigs.
This nose needs improving. It has to be flat."
She poked in pig nostrils. "It's perfect like that."

"Except for one detail," said Jillian Jiggs.
They lifted Rebecca, who added the twigs.

"Jillian, Jillian, look, look! They're gone!
Where are the mittens you used to have on?
You're in big trouble. When our mom finds out,
She'll fall down and faint, then she'll wake up and shout:

Jillian, Jillian, say it's not true!
How do you lose all the things that you do?"

They searched every cave, every hill, everywhere.
The mittens had gone, disappeared in thin air.

"Face it," said Rachel. "It's not the first time.
Your things just get lost. Don't stand there and whine."

Jillian smiled and blew her a kiss.
"My sleeves are long. I'll wear them like this."

"I'm ready," said Peter, "to try something new.
I've thought of another neat thing we can do.
We're here on Mars where the hills are so high,
I bet if we try them, our space sleds will fly!"

Peter was right. They zoomed down so fast,
All Mars was a blur as they hurtled past.

Swooping and looping, they dove and they dipped,
Not even stopping when they flopped or flipped.

It was then that her hat disappeared off her head.
"Oh no! Not again," poor Jillian said.

"You're in big trouble. When your mom finds out,
She'll fall down and faint, then she'll wake up and shout:

Jillian, Jillian, say it's not true!
How do you lose all the things that you do?"

They climbed up the hill and they searched with great care.
They shook every bush, but the hat wasn't there.

At last they gave up. They admitted defeat.
Besides, they were hungry. They needed to eat.

Jillian worried, "My mom will be mad.
How does it happen? I'm not REALLY bad."

Peter leaned over, whispering low.
"If she doesn't see you, then she'll never know."

"I'll tiptoe, like this, like a small quiet mouse.
She won't see a thing. I'll just sneak in the house."

She opened the door without making a noise,
Tiptoed inside, and then . . .

... tripped on her toys.

Her mother came running. "What happened?" she said.
And that's when she noticed her daughter's bare head.

"Jillian, Jillian, say it's not true!
You've lost your scarf, hat and both mittens, too?
What was it this time? Where did they go?"

"They're somewhere on Mars and they're buried in snow!"

# ~ ABOUT THE AUTHOR ~

**Phoebe Gilman** grew up in the Bronx, New York. From an early age she loved art, dancing, and books. Her mother got her a library card as soon as she could print her own name. She especially loved to read fairy tales, covering up the pictures with her hand if they didn't match what the words had painted in her head. She drew giant ballerinas on her bedroom walls.

When she was about ten years old, Phoebe illustrated her first book. It was written by her cousin Joel and was called *Oliver the Octopus*. Later, as part of a high school project, she illustrated *Chester the Chimponaut*. But it never occurred to her that she could grow up to be a writer and illustrator.

After studying art in high school and college, she lived in Europe and Israel and began a career as a fine artist, having exhibitions and selling her work. It wasn't until her older daughter was a toddler and lost a balloon in a tree that her thoughts turned to picture books again.

By this time Phoebe had moved to Toronto, Ontario, and was teaching at the Ontario College of Art. *The Balloon Tree* was published in 1984. She said: "Looking back, I can see all the pieces were there from the beginning. I had a mother who loved books and a cousin to invent stories and songs with. I learned to be a skilled artist, even if I didn't do it intentionally. If I had paid closer attention to what

my heart was whispering, perhaps I would have known sooner that what I love doing is making up stories and pictures to go with them. Certainly, I had enjoyed the making of *Oliver the Octopus* and *Chester the Chimponaut*. And when I had my own children, I loved to make up stories for them at night. I enjoyed the children's section of the library more than they did. Even the paintings that I did always told a story."

Phoebe once said that she wrote the books that she needed to read when she was growing up — tales of strong girls who outwit the bad guys and learn to follow their hearts. In addition to the Jillian Jiggs books and *The Balloon Tree*, she wrote and illustrated the bestselling *Something from Nothing*, which won the Ruth Schwartz Award and the Sydney Taylor Award; *Grandma and the Pirates*; *Little Blue Ben*; *The Gypsy Princess* and *Pirate Pearl*. She also illustrated *Once Upon a Golden Apple*, written by Jean Little. Her last book, *The Blue Hippopotamus*, illustrated by Joanne Fitzgerald, was published in 2007.

Phoebe Gilman died in 2002, but her stories continue to entertain and inspire children around the world.

# ~ ABOUT THE BOOKS ~

## JILLIAN JIGGS

"The idea for Jillian Jiggs came from a Mother Goose rhyme, Gregory Griggs:

*Gregory Griggs, Gregory Griggs:*
*Had twenty-seven different wigs.*

"I was going to have Gregory turn everything in the house into a wig, but I got stuck after the lampshade and the mop. Then I thought, why stop at wigs? Being the mother of two girls, I decided to use them as the models. Gregory's a rather peculiar name for a girl, so I had to change it. I couldn't find a three syllable girl's name that began with 'Gr.' The closest I could come to it was Gillian. So I dropped the 'r' from Griggs and Gillian Giggs was born. Once she arrived on the scene, she took over the story; why stop at wigs? Anything can be turned into a costume. Since the original inspiration for her story was a rhyme, it just continued in that format. But everyone was mispronouncing Gillian Giggs, so it was changed to Jillian Jiggs."

## THE WONDERFUL PIGS OF JILLIAN JIGGS

"This is a true story. Well — almost a true story. One day I showed my daughter Melissa how to make a little felt bookmark mouse. As soon as her friends saw it, they wanted one too. So Melissa went into business making mice. Each one was special. Each one was different. Each had a name. In the end, she couldn't part with any of them. I watched this happening and thought, "That's exactly what Jillian would do." I started to write and then I got stuck. *The Wonderful Mice of Jillian Jiggs* didn't sound right. It clunked! I gave up and put the story away. Weeks later, I awoke with a start. Jillian wouldn't make mice. She would make — PIGS!

"The rainbow picture on the cover was designed by my daughter Leora."

## JILLIAN JIGGS TO THE RESCUE

"This book started out to be about kids forming a club. The members of this club had to help others. The problem I had was to figure out who they could help. Why not Jillian's younger sister? What kind of problem could a little girl have? Why not a scary dream? By the time the story was finished, I had taken out all the club stuff because I didn't have enough room for it."

Only one thing in the book is left from that original idea — the club's secret password. You'll know it as the beginning of the monster-squishing rhyme: Kalamazoo!

## JILLIAN JIGGS AND THE SECRET SURPRISE

"*The Chicken Princess* play was actually written before the main story of the book. I originally thought that it could be published on its own. It is actually a lot longer than the other Jillian books. In fact, that was one of the problems with it. It had too many words for a picture book. It took many years for me to think up a good story to go with it."

The book is dedicated to Phoebe's granddaughters and her grand-nieces and grand-nephews — there are enough of them to put on a show of their own!

## JILLIAN JIGGS AND THE GREAT BIG SNOW

This story began with the memory of a special hat, covered with buttons, that once belonged to her daughter Melissa. Phoebe had a mental image of that long-lost hat, buried in a snowdrift, emerging in the spring thaw.

Phoebe actually made real versions of Jillian's Martian hat, to make sure that it would work: "When I tried to construct the propeller, it kept flopping over. I substituted something that looks like an old-fashioned TV antenna, which I made from the cut-off rim of a paper cup perched on top of a small tube. The whole business is covered with aluminum foil. I also made googly eyes from egg carton parts and added the spring antenna that I originally started with. Pretty soon, everyone will be wearing this chic construction."

## CAN YOU FIND?

When Phoebe Gilman was creating the first Jillian Jiggs book, she decided to hide a little bit of her first book, *The Balloon Tree*, in the illustrations. That started a tradition — she began hiding things from her previous books in every new one. Phoebe liked chickens, so every book also has at least one chicken in it, too. Here are just a few items to look for — but there are others, too. See what else you can spot!

### In *Jillian Jiggs*, look for:
- The wizard from *The Balloon Tree*
- A painting of thousands and millions and zillions of balloons
- Chickens

### In *The Wonderful Pigs of Jillian Jiggs*, look for:
- A picture from *The Balloon Tree*
- The book *The Balloon Tree*
- The Wizard's cat from *The Balloon Tree*
- A bit of the material of the dress from *Jillian Jiggs*
- Jillian's painted boxes
- The book *Little Blue Ben*
- A picture of Little Blue Ben
- The Blue Hen
- Painted chicks

### In *Jillian Jiggs to the Rescue*, look for:
- A painting of a balloon tree
- Jillian's dress from *Jillian Jiggs*
- Jillian's painted boxes
- Little Blue Ben
- Wonderful pigs
- The book *Grandma and the Pirates*
- The book *Once Upon a Golden Apple*
- The blanket from *Something from Nothing*
- A chicken

### In *Jillian Jiggs and the Secret Surprise*, look for:
- A balloon tree
- Jillian's painted boxes
- Mom's shoes from *Jillian Jiggs*
- Little Blue Ben (most of him is hidden)
- A wonderful pig
- Grandma from *Grandma and the Pirates*
- A golden apple
- Something made out of the blanket from *Something from Nothing*
- The kitten from *Jillian Jiggs to the Rescue*
- Babalatzzi the dancing bear from *The Gypsy Princess*
- Pirate Pearl's dog

### In *Jillian Jiggs and the Great Big Snow*, look for:
- A copy of *The Balloon Tree*
- Jillian's wings from *Jillian Jiggs*
- Little Blue Ben (he's really well hidden — look for his hair!)
- Jillian's pyjamas from *Jillian Jiggs to the Rescue*
- Wonderful pigs
- The Boss Pirate's hat from *Grandma and the Pirates*
- A golden apple
- The blanket from *Something from Nothing*
- Cinnamon and Babalatzzi from *The Gypsy Princess*
- Pirate Pearl and her dog